BEATEN

Suzanne Weyn

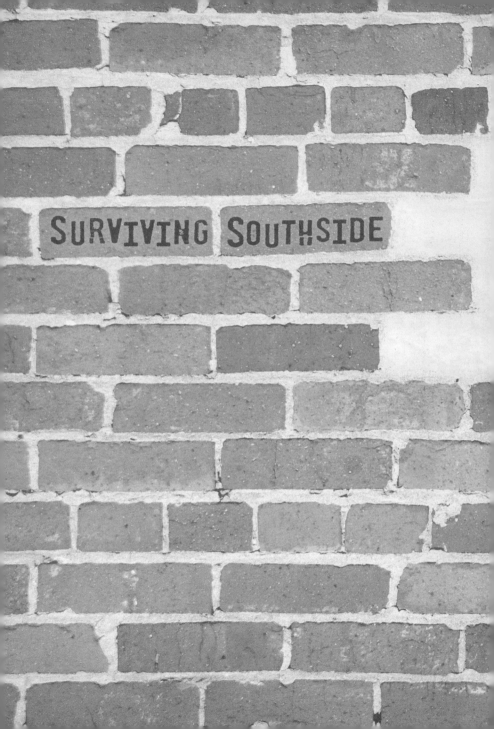

SURVIVING SOUTHSIDE

BEATEN

Suzanne Weyn

SCHOLASTIC INC.
New York Toronto London Auckland
Sydney Mexico City New Delhi Hong Kong

ISBN 978-0-545-40595-9

12 11 10 9 8 7 6 5 4 3 2   11 12 13 14 15 16/0

Printed in the U.S.A.   40

First Scholastic printing, September 2011

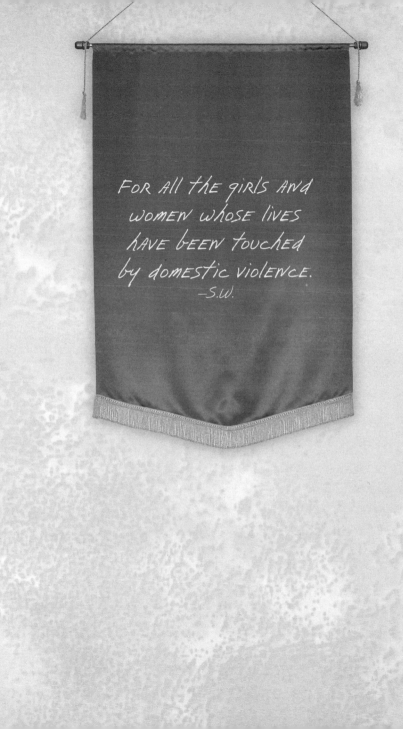

For all the girls and
women whose lives
have been touched
by domestic violence.
—S.W.

CHAPTER 1

"So it's official?" Ty asked. He put his arm up against the front door of my apartment building and leaned in closer. I couldn't tear my eyes away from his lips. "We're an item now, right?"

I had my back against the front door as I smiled up at him. Ty Hendricks is the star running back for our school's team, the Southside High Titans. So good-looking! He and I had been eyeing each other since

September this year. But it wasn't until the beginning of October that Ty had started walking home with me. We walked together every day for a full week before he finally went for a kiss. I'd wondered when he'd get to it.

"Is that what we are, an item?" I asked with a flirty grin.

He leaned in even closer so that I could detect the woodsy scent of his cologne. "You said you'd go with me, Paige. So, yeah, you're my girl now, right?"

"Mmm-hmm, I'm your girl," I confirmed, trying to play it cool.

Ty is not a real smiley guy. But when he does smile, it's like the sun coming out from behind a cloud. Beautiful and radiant!

I guess we're pretty opposite types. I'm bubbly and I talk to everyone. More than my athletic ability, that's probably the quality that got me elected captain of the cheerleading squad this year.

Ty's shy and intense. His teammates like him, though, and he's a real team player.

When he starts running down that football field, nobody can touch him.

Ty's face came close to mine, and I shut my eyes, getting ready for our lips to touch.

Bam! The front door banged into my back. It sent me crashing into Ty.

Ty staggered backward. Luckily, he's strong. He kept us both from being knocked down the front steps.

"Whoa! Sorry, you guys." It was my best friend, Sadie (short for Mercedes) who also lives in my building. She was still wearing her cheerleading outfit. "Why were you standing right in front of the door? That was kind of dumb."

"We were . . ." I looked into Ty's eyes ". . . talking."

"At least we were trying to," Ty added playfully.

"Oh, I see. Talking, huh?" she said knowingly. Sadie headed down the steps with a bounce. "Well, don't let me stop you from talking."

"No, wait, Sadie," Ty said. "I have to get home anyway. You stay and hang with Paige, if you want."

I frowned. Although I love Sadie to death, I did *not* want Ty running off so soon. This was a crucial moment. I had a kiss coming!

"Don't go," I said with a pout.

"Got to," Ty insisted as he headed down the steps. His movements were sure-footed and light. When he turned back, I was on the top step, sulking. I guess I was done playing it cool

Once more he shot me that gorgeous grin. In a flash he was back up beside me. He planted a warm kiss on my lips. Wrapping my arms around his broad shoulders, I returned it.

"I couldn't leave my girl unkissed," he said softly. "What was I thinking?"

"I don't know," I replied warmly. "I guess you weren't thinking at all."

"I guess not," he said, once more heading down the steps. He waved to Sadie and me.

"Call you tonight, Paige. Okay?"

"Call me," I agreed. "Don't forget."

"I won't."

CHAPTER 2

I was smiling so hard I thought my face might break as I turned to Sadie. "It's official. We're going out!" I reported gleefully. A giggle fizzed up in me like bubbles in a soda, and I clapped my hands with giddy delight. "Isn't he the best?"

Sadie kept her eyes on Ty as he disappeared down the street.

"Don't you think so?" I pressed her, my sunny expression starting to fade. I recognized that look on my friend's face, and I didn't like it.

"Yeah . . . I guess," Sadie replied without conviction.

I came down a couple of steps and stood next to her. "What? What's not to like about him?" I challenged.

"It's nothing really," Sadie said. "It's just that he seems . . . I don't know how to say it . . ."

"Just say it!" I snapped.

"It's hard to put into words. He was happy just now, but sometimes Ty seems wrapped a little tight, that's all."

A swell of anger washed over me, but I clamped down on it. I had asked for her opinion, after all. It wasn't Sadie's fault that I didn't like her answer. "What do you mean by wrapped tight?" I questioned.

Sadie shrugged her shoulders. "He's so . . . intense."

"What's wrong with being serious? One of the reasons he's so good at football is that he takes it seriously. He does well in school because he's a serious student, too. I don't see any problem with that."

Sadie gazed at my face, almost as if she was studying me. "I don't see you two together as a couple," she stated.

"Why not?"

"You're so happy and friendly. And he's . . . I don't know . . . not."

"You know what they say. Opposites attract," I told her. "I'm head cheerleader, and he's a star football player. I think we make the perfect couple."

And I truly believed that.

CHAPTER 3

Ty wasn't my first boyfriend, but I couldn't remember feeling so strongly about any other boy. We agreed about almost everything, from our opinions on who was going to make it to the Super Bowl to the kids and teachers we liked at school. We listened to the same music and watched the same TV shows. The same things struck us as funny. Despite what Sadie thought, Ty did have a sense of humor. During the next two weeks, we spent a lot of time talking.

One afternoon, as we were leaving school together, we were talking about what we'd be doing next year. I told him how nervous I felt about the whole process of applying to college. I'd taken one SAT. I'd done okay, but I wanted to see if I could get my score higher by taking it again.

"How are you planning to pay for college?" Ty asked me.

"My mom has some money saved," I said. "The rest will be loans and financial aid. I'm going to try to get some kind of job, too. How about you? I guess you'll be getting a football scholarship."

"I sure hope so," Ty replied. "My dad doesn't have any college fund set aside for me."

"Are you sure about that?" I asked.

He laughed darkly. "Absolutely sure."

This was the first time I'd ever heard Ty talk about either of his parents. I knew that his parents were divorced. His mother lived out in the suburbs. But it always struck me as odd that he never talked about either of them. I'd never even been to his apartment.

Ty's cell phone buzzed, and he glanced down at it, frowning.

"You're not going to answer it?" I asked.

Ty shook his head. "No. It's my dad. I've got to get home to help him with something right now, so I can't walk you to your place," he said.

"Will it take long? I could come with you."

"I don't know."

"Come on, please," I cajoled. "I want to meet your dad. Are you ashamed of me?" I teased.

"Are you kidding? It's just the opposite."

Was he saying he was ashamed of his dad?

"Please," I pleaded. "I've got to meet him sometime." I wanted to know everything about Ty and his family.

Ty looked away and seemed to be thinking about it.

"Oh, all right," he agreed. "Might as well get it over with."

As we headed for his apartment building, Ty grew quiet. I talked a mile a minute. I had a million questions, though something told me not to ask them. Ty's lips were shut tight, and his eyebrows were scrunched into a scowl.

Finally we stopped in front of Ty's apartment building. "Let me go up first," he suggested.

"Why?" I asked.

"Just to see how everything is. I'll be right back." Before I could say anything more, he headed on in, leaving me out on the sidewalk.

What was going on?

CHAPTER 4

I thought Ty would return in five, maybe ten, minutes. But twenty minutes later, I was still standing there. I started to wonder what was happening.

Two guys I knew from school came by and headed toward Ty's building. "Hey! Steve! Benito!" I greeted them. "Are you coming in here? Can you let me in?"

Steve turned to me. "Hey, Paige. You waiting for Ty?"

I nodded as Steve rang a buzzer for someone. When the door buzzed, he held the door for me.

"He was supposed to come down, but he's taking forever," I complained.

Steve exchanged glances with Benito.

"What?" I demanded.

"Ty's dad has a problem with the booze," Benito divulged. "Mr. Hendricks gets pretty nasty when he drinks."

"Why doesn't Ty go live with his mother?" I asked.

"Somebody has to look after Ty's dad, I guess. He used to beat up on Ty's mom and younger brother. I could hear it all the way down the hall when I was visiting my cousins. The cops were always here," Steve explained.

I got into the elevator with them. "Ty lives in 512," Steve said as they turned the other way.

When I got to apartment 512, I could hear a man shouting inside. The words he was using made me cringe. It wasn't so much his language but the fact that I could tell he was hurling his curses and insults at Ty. From behind the door I could hear Ty trying to calm him down.

Since I didn't know what to do, I just stood there. Suddenly the door flew open, and I was face to face with Ty.

I could see his father behind him.

"What are you doing here?" he shouted.

He had never raised his voice to me before!

"Sorry! Sorry!" he apologized immediately. "I just didn't expect to see you."

"Are you all right?" I asked urgently.

"Yeah, yeah. Let's get out of here," he replied, hurrying me back toward the elevator. He didn't say another thing until we were inside and headed down. "So, I guess you heard?"

"Just a little," I admitted. "Living with him must be really hard on you."

Ty wrapped his arms around me and pulled me close to him. "You have no idea, baby. No idea," he murmured, and I was sure I heard tears in his voice.

"It's okay, Ty," I reassured him, holding him tight. "I'm here for you. I won't ever leave."

Poor Ty. As I stood there with his arms around me, I wondered how he had turned out to be so wonderful, coming from such a horrible home life. It made me love him even more.

CHAPTER 5

By the first week of November, it looked like the Titans would have a real shot at the play-offs. Scouts from several colleges were starting to show up at practices.

"They were watching you," I told Ty excitedly during a break in one of the practices. "You're definitely going to get an offer."

Ty shook his head as he removed his helmet. "They're here to see Kadeem," he said, talking about Southside's star quarterback.

"And you," I insisted. "I saw them looking at you, too."

"You don't know what you're talking about, Paige," Ty snapped.

His tone of voice angered me. "I do so," I said. "I saw one guy point directly at you."

"Don't try to make me feel good," Ty said roughly.

I was about to reply when I was distracted by Lara Velez, another cheerleader. "Don't tell me the lovebirds are having a fight," she taunted with a flirtatious toss of her silky, dark hair. I did not like the way she smiled at Ty as she spoke.

"We're not fighting, and it's none of your business," I shot back. Lara is the biggest flirt on the squad and one of my least favorite people.

She ignored me and focused all her attention on Ty.

"Lookin' good out there, Ty," Lara crooned. "Those recruiters are going to be all over you. They're going to be throwing scholarships at you."

"You think so?" Ty replied. He seemed pleased to hear from Lara what he'd just barked at me for saying two minutes earlier.

A look of incredulous disbelief crossed my face as I stared at him. "I thought you said they were here for Kadeem," I reminded him.

Lara whirled around toward me. "What? You don't think Ty is every bit as good as Kadeem?" she said, acting as if she was shocked.

"That's not what I said," I defended myself. "Of course he's as good."

"That's not what you just said," Ty snarled.

"I didn't say that! You said it! I was just reminding you that—"

The coach blew the whistle signaling that practice was about to resume. "I've got to go," Ty grumbled, putting his helmet back on and running back to his teammates without even a wave good-bye.

"You should be more supportive of your boyfriend," Lara said smugly.

She tried to flounce off, but I wasn't going to let her have the last word. I hurried behind until I was alongside her, and then I got right in front, blocking her progress. "I am supportive of Ty. And you said it right, Lara—he's my boyfriend. So stay away."

"We'll see how long it lasts, Paige," Lara hissed before running off to join the other members of the cheer squad. I stood there fuming. Was something going on between Ty and Lara? Why had he been so short-tempered with me but just stood there and grinned at her? It hurt and confused me.

CHAPTER 6

For the rest of the scrimmage, Ty played brilliantly. As we practiced our cheers, I watched the scouts. They most certainly were studying Ty as well as Kadeem and a few other players. After every play, they checked stopwatches and made notes. Ty just refused to believe the recruiters were there to see him because he wanted a scholarship offer so badly. He didn't want to get his hopes up just to have them dashed.

After practice was over, Ty didn't even wait for me. Tears sprang to my eyes when I realized he wasn't standing outside the locker rooms where we usually met. This had never happened since we started going out.

I spied him at the end of the hall with a bunch of his teammates, but he didn't even look my way. I just hurried home. It was the first time I'd walked alone in weeks. All I could think about was getting into my room and shutting the door so I could let my tears fall freely.

When I neared my apartment building, I spied Ty standing out front. My heart skipped with joy, but then worry quickly overtook it. Had he come to break up with me? It had to be that. I was sure of it.

Every muscle of my body ached with tension as I walked up to him. I pressed my lips together, determined that he wouldn't see me cry.

"I'm sorry I was such a jerk, baby," Ty said, his hand reaching for mine.

I wasn't ready to forgive him so easily. He'd

really hurt my feelings. "Why didn't you wait for me?" I asked.

"I figured you were mad at me."

"I was!" I admitted. "Why did you talk to me like that?"

"I told you why! Paige, I'm an idiot. I don't blame you if you won't forgive me, but please say you will. You're the only one I can depend on these days. I took all my nerves out on you. I know you'll stand by me no matter what an idiot I am."

He really meant it. I could tell from the pained expression on his face. "That's the truth, Ty," I said softly. "I will stand by you, no matter what." And I meant it too.

Ty folded me in his arms. "I know, Paige. I know I can always count on you."

Lifting my head, I studied Ty's handsome face a moment before speaking. "Is there anything going on between you and that Lara?" I asked.

"Nothing," he assured me. "Not a thing. I was just being polite. With you, I can be myself."

"You can always be yourself with me, Ty."
I smiled at him. "Well, I guess it was bound to
happen. I think we just had our first fight."

CHAPTER 7

The note read: *I love you more than ever. Thanks for putting up with me.* I don't know which I loved more, the note or the bouquet of daisies in a glass. Ty had my locker combo, so both were sitting in my locker on Monday morning.

"What did you have to put up with to get those?" Sadie asked sourly as she read the note over my shoulder.

Normally, Sadie would have been the first

to know all about my little quarrel with Ty and how we had made up in just a few hours. But lately things between us hadn't been the same. She always had some negative remark to make about Ty, so I stopped talking to her about him.

"It wasn't anything much," I said, folding the note. "It was silly really. All couples fight sometimes."

"I guess so," Sadie allowed.

"I really hate to leave these flowers in the locker."

"Yeah, it would be a shame if the three dollars he spent on those were all for nothing," Sadie sniped.

"What is your problem?" I came back at her. "Why can't you ever say a nice thing about Ty? He brings me flowers, and for some reason you think that isn't good enough. What *is* good enough? Why can't you get off his case?"

"Why can't he get off mine?"

"What!?" I cried. "I don't know what you're talking about!"

"Oh, come on, you know Ty can't stand me."

"That is so not true!" I told her, though actually it was. Ty never wanted me to hang around with Sadie. But I couldn't blame him. Ty wasn't stupid. He could tell from the way she was always studying him with that suspicious glare of hers that she didn't trust him one bit.

"Don't lie to me, Paige," Sadie insisted. "Ty doesn't want you to be friends with me, does he?"

I folded my arms angrily. "Ty doesn't tell me who I can be friends with."

"How do you have time to be friends with anyone?" Sadie challenged. "You're with Ty every minute of the day."

"So? He's my boyfriend."

Sadie looked at me hard. "And I used to be your *best* friend."

Her words struck me like a hammer. "Used to be?" I asked.

Sadie threw her arms out from her sides. "Of course, used to be! You have no need for a best friend anymore. You have Ty!" Her face red, Sadie whirled away from me and stomped down the hall.

CHAPTER 8

I was frozen, mouth wide-open, as I watched her go. I hadn't realized my dating Ty had upset her that much. It was true, though, that I'd been neglecting our friendship. I'd told myself that Sadie was busy too, and wasn't missing me, but now I knew I had only been fooling myself.

"Something wrong?" I turned to face Ty, who had come up behind me.

My locker was still open, and I took the

daisies out. "Oh, Ty, they're beautiful!" I said, hugging him. "You didn't have to do this."

"Sure I did." He kissed me lightly on the lips. "Listen, I have to tell you the big news. The Titans are almost to the play-offs. If we win this weekend's game against Uniondale, we're in."

I jumped, pumping my fist in the air. "Scouts are bound to be there, and they'll all be watching you."

Ty took a folded piece of paper from his back pocket. Grinning, he showed it to me. The letterhead was from a school called Teller University. My eyes raced down the page. Once the meaning of the words sunk in, I threw my arms around Ty. "They want you to go there to a recruitment weekend! Ty, this is it! You're getting a football scholarship!"

"Teller has one of the best programs in the state," he told me happily. "We have to stay calm. I'm not in yet."

"Oh, but you will be. I know it! I just know it!"

"Thanks for believing in me, baby," Ty said, growing serious. "It means a lot."

"Of course I believe in you," I assured him honestly. "I believe in you so much that I'm going to apply to Teller University too."

That made Ty smile. "You don't even know what academic programs they have."

"I don't care," I said excitedly. "I'm sure it's a fine school, and all that matters is that we'll be together." I pictured the two of us walking together, hand in hand, across the Teller campus. I knew that once the play-offs came, my dream would become a reality.

CHAPTER 9

I was hoping I could fix things with Sadie. The Titans were putting in lots of extra practices and film sessions in preparation for the Uniondale game. That meant I had some free time to spare, since Ty was around much less.

Sadie didn't make it easy for me, though. When I called her cell, she wouldn't pick up. If I sent a text, she didn't text back. I even "poked" her on Facebook and received no response. She didn't come by my locker anymore, and I could never catch her eye, even during cheering sessions.

One afternoon, though, I ran into her in the hall of our apartment building. She was throwing a bag of trash down the garbage chute just as I was approaching to do the same. Sadie turned away quickly, but I called to her. "Don't run away, Sadie. Please. We need to talk."

"What's there to talk about, Paige?" She didn't even look at me.

"Our friendship."

"What about it? It's gone," Sadie stated coldly.

"I don't want it to be gone," I replied.

"Why? You have Ty to hang with."

"Come to my place and have a soda. Please?"

"Oh, all right," Sadie agreed reluctantly.

We sat at my kitchen table, and I finally got to tell her how badly I felt about ignoring her for Ty. "Why do you let him take up all your time?" Sadie asked. "Other girls have boyfriends, but they don't spend every second with them."

"I don't know," I admitted. "We just sort of got into the habit." I fiddled with the tab on my soda can. "Ty depends on me."

"For what?" Sadie asked. "He's a big boy. Can't he take care of himself?"

"Of course he can. It's just that his family is all messed up, and he counts on me to keep his spirits up when it gets him down. And his self-confidence isn't always so great. That's when he needs me the most."

"So you're his private cheerleader," Sadie said.

That sounded harsh, but there was probably some truth to it. "That's what you do when you love someone," I said in my own defense.

"And what does Ty do for you?" Sadie asked.

Me? I was so busy loving Ty that I had never stopped to think about what exactly Ty did for me. "I guess I don't need him to do anything," I said.

"Does he ever cheer you up when you're down?"

"I don't get down much, and I don't like to bother him with that stuff," I admitted.

"Do you think that's fair?" Sadie challenged.

Maybe it wasn't, but I had a sunnier disposition than Ty did. Plus, my family situation wasn't like his. My mom was a little annoying sometimes, but she was a good person. So was my dad, though I saw him a lot less often since they got divorced. Ty had much more to deal with. "Ty is a great boyfriend," I said, trying to sound confident. "He loves me and does the best he can."

I wanted to change the subject.

"That's why I need my best girlfriend back," I added with a smile. "Come on. Want to go to the movies tonight? That new romantic comedy is out. The one we read about in *People*."

"I know which one you mean," Sadie said, getting up from the kitchen chair. "Yeah, let's go. I have to babysit tonight but I could go right now."

"Okay. I'm going to change, and then I'll come get you," I agreed, waving as she headed to my front door. I grinned, happy we were friends again.

CHAPTER 10

My special Ty ringtone sounded, and I clicked into his call. "Hey, baby," I greeted him. "Ready for your big recruitment weekend?"

"Paige, I need your help."

I shifted uncomfortably in my chair. "Sure, Ty. What's wrong?"

"My father was supposed to drive me to Teller this afternoon, but he's passed out drunk on the couch."

"Oh, no! Can you go in the morning?"

"I could, but there's supposed to be a big party tonight where all the coaches meet the recruits. If I miss it, they won't even know who I am for the scrimmage."

"Well, what can you do? Is there anyone you can catch a ride with?"

"Everyone's left already," Ty replied. "I was hoping maybe I could catch a bus."

"That's a great idea," I said.

"Can you take me to the bus station, Paige?" Ty asked. "I've never been on a bus. I don't know my way around the bus station."

I hesitated. "It's just that I made plans to go to the movies with Sadie right now."

"And that's more important than helping me out?" Ty said, sounding hurt.

"No, no, of course not. I'll just call her to cancel. Meet me outside my building. Don't worry. We'll get you there in time for the party."

— — — — —

By the time I arrived at school on Monday morning, I was in a foul mood. When I'd called to tell Sadie why I couldn't go to the movies with her, she got really mad at me. She said she should have known that I would put Ty ahead of our friendship. I got angry right back at her for not understanding that this was a special situation.

On top of that, Ty had been gone all weekend, and I missed him. We got him onto his bus okay, but I could tell he was really uptight about the weekend. While he was away, he didn't pick up any of my calls. Once he sent me a text that read: *Really busy. Talk to you Mon.* After that, I didn't try to get in touch with him anymore. It surprised me a little that I didn't even hear from him Sunday night when he got home. And when I called him, he didn't answer.

CHAPTER 11

As soon as I finished at my locker, I headed straight to Ty's. The minute I spied him taking his books out, I put aside my gloomy mood and planted a smile on my face. "So, how did it go?" I asked, cotming up alongside him. "I bet they were amazed when they saw you. Did they offer you a scholarship then and there? I suppose that's too soon, but—"

"Could you stop jabbering?"

I stepped back, almost as if he'd slapped me. "What?"

"Would you stop babbling?"

"Ty, what's the matter?"

Ty slammed his locker shut with a bang. "I'm tired of you talking all the time. You didn't even give me a chance to answer you."

"Sorry," I said, my feelings hurt. "Tell me how it went."

"Terrible. I got there just as the party was ending. I did horribly at the scrimmage, which didn't matter because none of the scouts seemed to know who I was anyway."

"You probably did better than you think you did," I suggested cheerfully.

"Paige, don't be idiotic. You weren't even there!"

"I know you're a good player, Ty."

"Well, I wasn't any good that day."

We were supposed to be in class already. The halls were almost empty, but I didn't feel I could just leave Ty at that moment, not when he felt as awful as he did.

"You're probably just tired from the weekend," I said. "Do you want to ditch class and go to the diner?"

"Yeah, maybe," Ty agreed sullenly.

Turning back to his locker, we both stuffed our books inside. We had to move fast before a teacher came along and issued us a detention slip for not being in class. We didn't talk again until we were down by the gym locker rooms.

In a few more minutes we had crossed the athletic fields and were out on the street. I let out a quick sigh of relief. We'd made it.

Looking up at Ty, I scowled. His face was pinched into an expression of worry. His head was down and his shoulders were hunched. "Ah, come on, cheer up, baby," I said brightly, taking his hand. "I'm sure you were great."

"I wasn't," he grumbled.

"Yes, you were," I insisted lightly. I tickled him under his chin. "Don't look so serious. You can give me a little smile, can't you?"

"Stop doing that," Ty snarled.

I tickled him again, this time under his armpit. "Nuh-uh, not until you smile."

"Quit it, would you?"

"Just smile for me," I pleaded, pretending to pout. "Give me one itsy-bitsy smile." I tickled his cheek.

"I said quit it!" With a swipe of his muscular arm, Ty slapped me aside.

CHAPTER 12

My cheek burned from the slap as my feet slid out from beneath me. In the next second, the side of my face hit the cement. Then my shoulder. And then my hip and legs crashed onto the sidewalk.

For a moment, I was too stunned to do anything, even move.

I didn't want to cry, but it was an automatic reaction. They weren't big sobs, but tears ran down my cheeks before I could even stop them.

"Oh, God, Paige! I'm so sorry!" Ty was stooped beside me, helping me into a sitting position. "How do you feel? Do you think anything's broken?"

My jeans had ripped, and I could see my leg was scraped and bleeding. My face and neck throbbed where I'd hit the ground. When I touched my stinging cheek, my hand came back with blood on it.

"I'm so sorry, Paige. I'll take you to the hospital," Ty offered.

"No," I declined, wiping tears from my eyes. "I'm okay."

Slowly I began to get back onto my feet, but Ty held me down. "Sit a minute. Make sure you're all right. That's a nasty gash on your leg. How's your head?"

"It hurts," I admitted.

"Oh, baby, I . . . I . . ." Ty's voice caught in his throat, and he turned his face away from me. "I would never hurt you. You know that, right?"

I wanted to say, *but you just did.* It didn't seem like the right thing to say, though. When

Ty looked at me again there were tears in his eyes.

"You told me to stop tickling you. I should have listened. It wasn't your fault," I heard myself say.

"No, it was my fault. You just caught me wrong on a bad day. That's all. There's no excuse for what I did. It will never happen again. I promise you that."

"I know it won't, Ty. I'm sorry I got you so mad." I didn't want to make things worse and upset him even more when it was clear that he already felt terrible.

━━ ━━ ━━ ━━ ━━

"What happened to you?" My mom asked when she saw my scrapes and bruises. I told her we'd been working on a cheer move involving a pyramid, and I'd fallen from the top spot. "Your poor face," she said, dampening a cloth in the kitchen sink to clean me up. "You're bleeding."

Mom insisted on having a doctor check me

at the hospital emergency room. They cleaned my scrapes, ran a few tests, and concluded that I seemed okay. A doctor told Mom to watch for the signs of a concussion.

CHAPTER 13

The big game against the Uniondale Cougars was scheduled for the following Saturday. The entire school was jazzed for it. Posters that read GO TITANS and CLOBBER THE COUGARS were hanging all over the school.

Our cheer coach called for extra practices so we could learn all sorts of new moves. I'm usually a flier, which means I'm the one who gets tossed from the top of the pyramid by the ones below, called the bases. Sadie was a base. I knew she would never intentionally drop me, no matter how angry she was. What made me nervous was that Lara was also a base.

I was so stiff and achy from my fall that it was hard for me to keep up. At one practice, I stumbled after turning a cartwheel because my leg hurt so badly. "Did Ty do that to you?" Lara Velez jeered, pointing to the ugly purple bruise around the scabbed-over scrape on my leg.

"No! Who told you that?" I snapped defensively.

"Who could blame him if he did?" Lara went on.

I opened my mouth to reply, but nothing came out. Was she saying that if Ty hurt me I deserved it? Lara stood there smirking obnoxiously, and I didn't want to let her taunt me into a fight. "He didn't hurt me," I repeated feebly, rubbing my shin. "He didn't."

"Well, you had better be careful when you do the jump from the pyramid. You don't look too steady on your feet," Lara remarked. Her tone of voice made me wonder if it was a threat.

I noticed Sadie watching me with a worried expression. When our eyes met, she turned away, though. I really wished I could talk to her about Ty. All that week he'd been distant and sullen. It was as though everything I said aggravated him. "Just give me some space," he advised me. "I'm under a lot of pressure with this game. Everything is riding on it. Just back off me for a while, and I'll be all right once this is over."

Backing away from Ty wasn't easy for me. For the past weeks I'd spent all my time with him. Now, when I called him, he sounded annoyed. "I told you I need to focus on the game right now," he'd say. Or he would tell me again to give him more space.

I tried to be sensible about it. After all, it wouldn't be for long. But I suddenly felt all alone. I was used to Ty needing me. It was upsetting that he didn't want me around all of a sudden. And neither did Sadie. Ever since I had blown off our trip to the movie, she'd been giving me the cold shoulder.

At home, I was moping on the couch when Mom came and sat beside me. "You okay?" she asked.

I shrugged and leaned into her shoulder. It seemed like a long time since I'd talked to her, too. Lately all my "mom and me" time had gone to Ty. "Ty's busy with football practice, and Sadie is mad at me," I divulged.

"Why is she mad?" Mom asked.

I told her the whole story, and she listened without interrupting. "Maybe it's good that he's not around so much," she said when I was finished.

I sat back and stared at her. "Why do you say that?"

"He takes up all your time, Paige. You need a life of your own, too. Everything can't be about Ty. What about you?"

"I have a life," I insisted. "My grades are good, and I'm head cheerleader. That's about all I have time for."

"What about friends?"

"I told you, Sadie's not speaking to me."

"Other friends besides Sadie," Mom said.

"I have the cheer squad."

"Mmm, I suppose." Mom didn't seem convinced. She patted my knee as she got up from the couch. "I just don't want Ty to smother you or hold you back."

I couldn't believe what I was hearing. "I don't know why you would say that," I told her.

"Well, what about this application you made to Teller University? Why do you suddenly want to go there? It doesn't offer any program you're interested in. Is it because Ty is going there?"

"It's a great school, and I don't know what I want to do yet."

"I thought you were interested in fashion design."

"I told you, I'm not sure."

Both of us were starting to raise our voices, and I really was not in the mood to fight with her. "Forget it. You don't understand," I grumbled as I got up from the couch and headed toward my room. "You don't really know me or Ty."

CHAPTER 14

The day of the big game finally came. On the morning of the game, Cougars-vs.-Titans fever was burning red-hot all over school. I had it, too. I was sure that with Kadeem as our quarterback and Ty as the running back, we just couldn't lose. "I'm going to be so proud when I see you out there scoring touchdown after touchdown," I told Ty when I met him at his locker.

"Don't pressure me," Ty snapped.

"What?"

"I'm tense enough, and now you're expecting me to score all these touchdowns. Why? You want to look good in front of all the other cheerleaders? Oh, look at my boyfriend; he's making all the touchdowns."

I stared at him in disbelief. "Are you crazy?"

"Me, crazy? What about you? You're the one insisting I have to be the star of the team."

"I was only saying I was sure you would do well tonight," I told him, a note of anger in my cold voice.

"I don't need the added pressure, okay? I'm tense enough as it is," he replied.

It was clear that he wasn't kidding. Every muscle in his body, including those in his face, was taut. He reminded me of a rubber band stretched to its limit, one that was about to snap at any second.

"You know what? I can't wait for this game to be over. Then maybe you can get back to being your old self," I said. "When we go to the after-game party and you're finally calmed down because we won the game, I will be so happy."

"What party?" Ty asked, closing his locker.

"The one the Pep Squad is holding in the gym."

"I'm not going," Ty stated firmly. He headed down the hall without even waiting for me.

I hurried alongside him. "Why not?"

"I won't be in the mood."

"Yes, you will. Why wouldn't you be? If we win, you'll want to celebrate. And if we lose . . . well . . . we won't lose."

"Quit bugging me about it, Paige. Just leave me alone."

CHAPTER 15

The game was at Uniondale. The night was cold, and my breath came out in small misty clouds. The bright lights were so intense that I couldn't even see the stars in the clear, dark sky above us.

The stands were packed with fans from both teams. Glancing up at the bleachers from where the cheer squad had assembled, I searched for Ty's father but didn't see him.

I ran out onto the field with the cheerleading squad, and we did our opening routine. It went well, and the crowd applauded our pyramid. My heart pounded when it was time for the jump. Was this the moment Lara would let me fall? But Lara, Sadie, and another base named Kim caught me.

When it was time for the Titans to take the field, I jumped up and waved my pom-poms over my head. "Go Titans! Go Ty!" I shouted. I was hoping for a smile and a wave, but instead Ty kept his head down as he followed his teammates out. To say I was disappointed would be an understatement, but I told myself Ty was focused on the game and I shouldn't have broken his concentration.

In the first quarter, Kadeem was about to be sacked when he lateraled the ball to Ty. It looked like Ty had a straight shot at the end zone, and the Southside fans started shouting and cheering like crazy. But this seemed to distract Ty. He slowed a bit just before the goal line and without realizing it veered into the path of two defenders.

In seconds, the Cougars tackled him to the ground.

Throughout the first two quarters, I watched as Ty was tackled time after time. He hadn't scored one touchdown or even caught a pass for a first down yet. He was off his game, even though his teammates were picking up the slack.

By the end of the second half, the score was tied. The game went into overtime. Fans on both sides were shouting themselves hoarse. I was also on the verge of losing my voice. The atmosphere was electric with excitement.

The Cougars scored a touchdown, and their side went wild.

The Titans had four downs to tie it up again.

The Cougars managed to contain Ty and Kadeem for the first three downs. With their season on the line, Kadeem threw a short pass to Ty, who leaped into the air and snagged the ball over the head of a defender. He had a couple of teammates blocking as the Cougars came after him, but several defenders broke through and gained on Ty.

Ty juked left and dodged right as he muscled toward the end zone, but with only a couple of yards to go, he was dragging two defenders. A third Cougar hit Ty hard, and he went down at the one-yard line. Even worse, Ty lost the ball as he hit the ground.

The Cougars had won!

I stared at Ty, who was still lying on the field. Why didn't he get up? Was he hurt?

The coach and the other Titans were headed in his direction when Ty pulled himself up into a sitting position and slowly climbed to his feet.

I sighed with relief, happy that he was okay.

But as Ty slouched his way off the field, head down, I could see, even from half a football field away, that he was completely miserable.

CHAPTER 16

I stood outside the boys' locker room, waiting for Ty. Almost everyone else had left, heading over to the party at Southside's gym. Win or lose, the Pep Squad was holding the event either way.

Kadeem came out of the locker room and cast a weary smile at me. "Waiting for Ty?" he asked.

I nodded. "What's taking him so long?"

"He's taking the defeat hard, like it's his fault alone."

"Oh, no!" I said. "I had a feeling that's what he was doing."

"The guy's hard on himself," Kadeem said. "He didn't play his best game tonight, but, hey, it happens. It was probably nerves. Sometimes you can want something too much, you know?"

"Could you tell him I'm waiting?" I asked.

Kadeem shouted inside for Ty to get a move on. Uniondale was going to lock up soon. "And you don't want to miss the Better Luck Next Year party. Free food, man! You can drown your sorrows in ginger ale." He turned back to me. "He's coming. See you over there, Paige."

"Thanks," I replied with a wave.

In a few minutes Ty emerged from the locker room. "Don't say anything chirpy and positive, Paige. I don't think I can take it. Let's not talk, okay?"

"Okay," I agreed. "We're going over to the party, right?"

"What for?" he barked roughly. "So everyone can look at the guy who blew our chance to go to the play-offs? So they can tell me it wasn't my fault when they all know it was?"

"That's not true, Ty. You're a team and the team—"

"Paige, I asked you not to!" he snapped. "Come on, get in the car. I'll take you home."

"I want to go to the party," I insisted.

"Without me?"

"Yes. I can do things without you. I have my own mind."

"Are you looking for some new guy? I guess you don't want to be with a loser like me anymore. You only wanted to be with a football star. Miss Head Cheerleader with the star running back. Now the picture's not so perfect, and you want to go find a new guy, right? Why don't you go over to the Cougars' party? You'll find some happy winners over there."

I stared at him as if he was a stranger. "Have you lost your mind?" I asked.

"No, just the opposite. I see you clearly for the first time." He swung out the door, letting it close before I got there. Hurrying into the almost empty parking lot, I looked around for someone else who could give me a ride to the party, but I didn't see anyone I knew.

"Are you coming?" Ty shouted from beside his car.

I hurried over and got in. "Just take me home."

"Whatever," he said, starting the engine.

CHAPTER 17

Ty and I sat in silence as he pulled out of the parking lot and into the street. We were stopped at a red light when his cell phone sounded. He took the phone out of his jacket, glanced at it, and smiled, just a little.

"Who's that?" I asked as the light turned green and he drove on.

"Nobody."

"Tell me," I demanded. If it was nobody, why wouldn't he tell me?

"None of your business."

He'd put his phone in his jacket pocket, and I quickly reached in and snatched it out. "Give me that!" he yelled, trying to grab the phone back from me with his right hand while he drove with his left.

It was from Lara. While he flailed at me, I hunched into the corner of the seat by the door and read: Where r u? C u you at the party.

I pushed Ty's arm away from me. "You're meeting Lara at the party?" I accused angrily.

"I'm not going to the party."

"Is that so? Then why did she write this?"

"How should I know?" he cried.

"You just wanted to get rid of me so you could go back to the party and be with Lara," I shouted. "Fine! Let her put up with you. Pull over. I'm getting out of the car."

Ty kept driving, ignoring me.

"I said, pull over to the curb. I am getting out of this car."

"Sit still and shut up!" he barked. "I'm taking you home."

We came to another red light, and I opened the door and got out. I couldn't stand to sit next to him for another second. I'd put up with so much from Ty, and now he was cheating on me with Lara. It was more than I could stand.

I heard Ty shouting for me to get back in the car as I crossed to the sidewalk. Good! I was free of him once and for all. I could see a bus stop in front of an apartment building about a half block down, and I headed for it, walking fast.

Ty pulled up to me and got out of the car. "Get back in the car," he commanded. Like he had the right to tell me what to do!

"Go away!" I told him angrily. "I've had enough of you. Just leave me alone."

Ty grabbed my arm hard. It hurt. "Get in the car!" he demanded.

"You're hurting me! Let go!"

"Not until you get in the car!"

He began pulling me toward the car, but I was determined not to let him. I shoved him back hard with my shoulder, and as he released me he tottered backward into a street sign and hit his head.

He cursed at me, and a frightening, enraged expression twisted his face. He lunged forward, and the next thing I knew I was on the ground with my arms over my head to shield myself as he slapped me hard over and over, calling me awful names.

I begged him to stop, but my head spun as he delivered a blow that split my lip. It felt like it would never end.

"You there! Stop! I've called the police!" Ty spun around and saw an elderly man talking on a cell phone. With the lightning speed of the running back that he was, Ty bolted down the street to his car. He peeled out into the road and, with squealing tires, raced off.

I sat on the sidewalk, sobbing. The man came to my side and squatted beside me. "Don't worry, young lady. The police are on their way. They'll take care of you. Can I call anyone for you?"

I wanted to ask him to call my mother, but all I could do was cry.

CHAPTER 18

Everything that happened after that seems hazy to me now. The police came with an ambulance, and I was put on a stretcher and lifted into the back. The ambulance raced to the hospital with the siren screaming. My mother was waiting when they arrived.

The nurses gave me some pain medication that made me very sleepy. I think I dozed on and off as they cleaned me up, put a few stitches in my forehead after administering a local anesthetic, and taped my sprained wrist. They took X-rays and checked me all over. Because one doctor said I was in shock, they wrapped me in warm blankets and gave me more pills. The doctor had me stay the night so they could keep watch over me in case something unexpected developed.

In the middle of the night, I awoke from a nightmare, and for a second I didn't know where I was. Then I saw Mom sleeping in a chair beside my bed. The moonlight was shining in through the blinds and onto her hair. All the events of the past night came back to me, and silent tears rolled down my cheeks.

In the morning, while I was eating my hospital breakfast with Mom, two uniformed police officers, a man and a woman, came into the room. "We have the young man who assaulted your daughter in custody," said the woman named Officer Ramirez, speaking to Mom. "Do you intend to press charges against Tyler Hendrickson?"

"Yes," Mom said instantly.

"No!" I spoke at the same time as Mom.

"Paige, he beat you up," Mom said to me, her tone rising with indignation.

"I know, but an arrest will ruin his life," I pointed out.

Mom turned to the officers. "I am definitely pressing charges."

"Mom, no. Please!" I begged her. "You can't!" If Ty was arrested, he'd never get his football scholarship. He wouldn't be able to go to college. "It was a bad night, and he lost his temper. He didn't mean it. Officers, I don't want to press charges."

"You're a minor child. We have to abide by your mother's wishes," Officer Ramirez told me.

"Press charges," Mom insisted.

Mom had to sign a release saying the police could use my medical report as evidence. The male officer wrote something on a pad, and they left, saying they would be in touch.

"Mom, why did you do that?" I asked unhappily.

Taking a compact mirror from her purse, Mom held it in front of my face.

"That boy did this to my baby girl," she said in a voice choked with emotion. What I saw in the mirror wasn't pretty. I had black-and-blue bruises over half my face, and my bottom lip was three times its normal size.

I suddenly realized that my body ached all over. But worse than that—worst of all my injuries—my heart hurt, like it had been broken into a million pieces.

CHAPTER 19

I stayed home for the next three days. Sleeping and crying were my two main activities. My busted lip made it too painful to eat much. At first, my body was stiff and ached even more than it had in the hospital, but slowly I began to feel better.

Late in the afternoon of the third day, my cell phone sounded with Sadie's ringtone. "Hey," I greeted her feebly.

"How are you? I heard what happened."

"Has everyone heard?" I asked.

"Pretty much, yeah," Sadie admitted sheepishly. "It's been all over Facebook, and everybody's been tweeting about it. It's gone like wildfire through the school."

"It has?" That's when I realized Mom had been shielding me from it, keeping my phone and not letting me use the computer. "What are people saying?"

"Everyone feels terrible and hopes you're okay. The cheer squad sent you a card that you'll probably get today."

"That's nice," I said. We talked some more, and I learned that Ty was out of jail on bail, but that he was suspended from school until his court date. He had been ordered by a judge not to have any contact with me.

"When can you come back to school?" Sadie asked.

"As soon as I feel better," I told her. Knowing I wouldn't run into Ty made me more willing to return. I figured he must be furious at me for having him arrested.

He probably wouldn't even believe it wasn't something I had wanted.

On the morning of the fourth day, I borrowed some of Mom's heaviest foundation makeup and went to work covering my purple bruises. A lot of the swelling had gone down, though my lip still looked pretty ugly. I figured everyone already knew what had happened, anyway.

That morning, Sadie was waiting for me down in the lobby. We walked to school together, and I appreciated that she didn't say much. I wouldn't have known what to tell her because I hadn't sorted out my feelings. Although it seemed unbelievable, even to me, part of me missed Ty. It was as though I'd split him into two people—hurtful, violent Ty and vulnerable, sensitive Ty. It was my sweet, understanding boyfriend that I wanted to see again, not the uptight, enraged, shadow Ty lurking below the surface.

Just before we were about to enter the school building, Sadie put her hand on my arm to stop me. "I wasn't sure if I should tell you this or not, but there's something I think you should know."

The look of distress on her face alarmed me. "What?"

"Lara has posted some nasty stuff on her Facebook profile, and some other kids have commented. She said that you deserved what you got."

I was stunned. Was it possible that Lara could even be that low? "What kind of comments?"

"A lot of kids said that she was crazy."

"But not everyone?" I pressed.

Sadie shook her head unhappily. "Ty has a lot of friends who can't believe he would do something like that. They posted comments saying you probably started it or did something so bad that you drove him to it."

"Are you kidding?"

"I'm sorry, but no. There are even kids who say you're lying."

That made me laugh scornfully. "Like I did this to myself? Come on."

"One kid suggested that you got drunk and fell, and you're trying to put the blame on Ty because he was about to leave you for Lara."

"Who said that?" I demanded. My mind was reeling from all this. Why would people say such things?

"A friend of Lara's, of course."

"Of course."

Facing the school's front doors, I suddenly felt a lot less eager to go in.

"Not everyone is saying those things," Sadie added. "I just thought you should be aware of what some people have said."

"Thanks," I told her as I headed in, feeling as though I had been beaten up all over again.

And yet . . . a small voice in my head was asking if maybe there wasn't just a little bit of truth in what they were saying about me.

CHAPTER 20

The next time I saw Ty was in the courtroom. There were no jurors, just a judge, a woman in her fifties with tied-back black hair and a stern expression. Her name plate read "Judge Estelle Santiago."

Ty was seated at a table up front with his lawyer—a bald man in a gray suit. I was a little surprised that his father wasn't there. But I was realizing that Mr. Hendrickson was not there most of the time.

My mother and I sat on the other side of the aisle, behind the prosecutor, a woman with short white hair, also in a suit. I stole a sideways glance at Ty. He looked thinner and very, very sad.

My lawyer called the kind man who had come to my aid that night as a witness. He smiled at me as he went to take the stand, and I returned his smile. I felt so grateful to him for helping me. I had to admit that if he hadn't come along and gotten involved I could have ended up in much worse shape than I was.

He told the judge what he'd seen that night, how he heard me beg Ty to stop. "That kid was not going to let up, though," he testified. "If I hadn't told him I'd called the police, who knows when he would have quit hitting her?"

Ty was the next to tell his side of the story. Going to the stand, he looked at me for the first time. I was afraid that he would be filled with rage about his arrest, but instead his expression was soft and full of apology. There was so much remorse and pain in his face that it went straight to my heart.

On the stand, Ty cried as he spoke. He explained how badly he'd played at the game and how worthless it had made him feel. "If I could take that night back, I would give anything," he said. "I hate myself for hurting the best girl in the world. She was just trying to cheer me up, but I was so angry at myself for blowing the game that I took it out on her. The beating I gave her was meant for me. She caught the pounding I wanted to give to myself." He broke down into sobs and then lifted his face to speak directly to me. "I'm so sorry, Paige. You've got to believe me."

Mom murmured under her breath. "Of course he's sorry now. He's about to go to jail."

Her expression was rock hard, but I didn't feel the same. I knew what pressure he'd been ·under. She didn't understand him like I did: how sweet he could be, how tough his life at home was.

I took the stand next. My lawyer mentioned what my mother had told her—that I'd come home bruised before. I admitted that Ty had caused the injuries. "So this wasn't the first time he'd assaulted you," she prompted.

"No, but the other time he didn't mean to hurt me, it just happened," I answered.

"It just happened because he was angry?"

"Well, yeah."

"I see."

She got me to describe the events of the night. It was painful to even talk about them. My lawyer showed Judge Santiago the medical records from that night and some photos of my injured face and other bruises that I hadn't even realized were being taken. The judge cringed when she looked at them.

"I know that looks bad," I said, speaking directly to Judge Santiago, "but I knew Ty felt bad, and I just kept talking to him when he asked me not to. I should have gotten back into the car with him. He only wanted to take me home, and if I hadn't given him such a hard time, none of this would have happened."

Judge Santiago stared at me with a hard expression. There was a strange sadness in her eyes. "So, you're saying that the beating you endured at the hands of Tyler Hendrickson was your own fault?"

"In a way," I admitted.

The judge shook her head wearily. "You poor girl," she said.

Glancing at Mom, I saw the same weariness on her face.

The judge then issued her decision. "In view of the defendant's age and because this is his first offense, I order Tyler Hendrickson to five years of probation and five hundred hours of community service."

Ty didn't register any emotion, but I was happy he wouldn't be going to jail. I couldn't help smiling just a bit.

"During the next five years, during the term of his probation, the defendant is not to see or speak to Paige Martin either in person, by phone, or by electronic media, for any reason whatsoever," Judge Santiago continued. "An attempt to make contact with Ms. Martin will be viewed by the court as a breach of the terms of probation and may be punishable by the issuance of jail time."

Not see Ty for five years! I'm sure my distress was written across my face.

Judge Santiago turned to my mother and our lawyer. "I am also ordering Paige Martin into court-mandated counseling. I want this young lady to have somebody to talk to before this happens to her again."

CHAPTER 21

Ty broke his probation the very next night. Just before I was about to go to bed, he called my cell. I hesitated only a second before taking the call. I just couldn't resist.

"Paige, thanks for picking up. Can I come see you?"

My heart raced. I wanted to see him so badly. I could tell I was talking to the sweet Ty, the one that I loved. "But you'll get in trouble," I objected.

"I don't care. No one will know. Meet me on the corner by the ice cream store."

"I shouldn't," I said, worried.

"Come on, please."

"All right. I'll be there in ten minutes." I knew Mom was asleep already. I could slip out and be back before she ever knew I was gone.

When I arrived at the corner, Ty was waiting in the dark alley between Harry's ice cream store and a Dunkin' Donuts. "Paige," he called to me.

It took me a moment to see him leaning against the wall, dressed in his varsity jacket and jeans. I joined him there in the shadows.

He studied my face, running his fingertips gently over my bruises. "I'll never hurt you again, Paige. I swear it. Do you believe me?"

I nodded, but would I ever be able to forget what had happened? I wanted to believe we could put it behind us.

Ty fished some dollars from his back pocket. "Go get us two milkshakes," he said, handing me the money. "Then we can take them into the park and sit on a bench. No one will notice us there."

I bought the shakes, and we went into the nearby park and walked along the paved path, looking for a place to sit. "Are you willing to see me again?" Ty asked.

"It will have to be a secret," I reminded him.

"So we'll meet in secret."

"If we both go to Teller next year, no one there will even know about us," I suggested. "We won't even have to hide."

Ty looked at the ground and shook his head. "I'm not going to Teller. I haven't gotten any offers. After the way I played at Uniondale, I'm not surprised. I'm pretty sure the recruits all heard about me being arrested, too."

"I'm sorry," I said.

"It's okay. I heard you in court. I know it wasn't your idea. I know it was all your mother's fault."

"Well, she was just looking out for me," I defended her.

"Yeah, sure, and she's probably just another man-hater, like my mother."

"No, she's not," I insisted. I didn't like him saying that about her. And from what I knew of his father, I could understand how his mother might feel, too. "Don't say that about my mother."

"Oh, so you think what she did was right?" he challenged.

"I didn't want her to press charges, but she doesn't hate men." As I spoke, my heel caught in a crack in the cement. I stumbled, and my shake flew from my hands and splashed onto his jacket.

"My jacket!" he cried angrily, looking down at the mess there. "It's ruined."

The expression of anger on his face suddenly brought me back to that horrible night. Had I once more made him so angry that he was going to hit me? And here I was, alone in the park with him? What if no kindly stranger came along this time?

I backed away from Ty. "I'm sorry, Ty. I didn't mean to do that. I have to go. I'm really sorry, but I can't do this. I can't see you any more."

Leaving my empty shake cup on the sidewalk, I turned and ran back up the pathway. Knowing Ty was a lot faster than me, I pumped my feet hard, expecting him to tackle me to the ground at any moment.

I didn't stop running until I was outside my apartment door, my back against the wall, panting heavily. Only then did I realize that Ty hadn't come after me. If he had, he'd have caught me.

And I had another realization, as well. I could never have a relationship with Ty again. I was too afraid of him.

CHAPTER 22

I didn't hear from Ty again for the rest of the week, and he didn't seem to be back at school. But on the following Monday, I was turning a hallway corner on my way to the guidance office when I came upon Ty and Lara kissing in the hall.

My heart froze, and a shot of deep hurt ran through me. But as I hurried by, I found myself worrying about Lara. Sure, we weren't friends, but I didn't want her to catch the same kind of beating I had. She didn't deserve that, no matter how obnoxious she was.

I arrived at the guidance office just in time for my Victims of Domestic Abuse group session. Four other young women from my school were there and one guy. Three of them, like me, had been hurt by their boyfriends. One was there because she'd seen her father beat her mother for years. The fifth one, the guy, had come because he saw his mother shoot his father. His head was seriously messed up.

The counselor, Ms. Phillips, met with all of us in her office. There was another woman there, a really beautiful tall woman with black curls that fell gracefully to the shoulders of the beige linen poncho she wore above a skirt and boots.

"We have a guest today," Ms. Phillips told us. "This is Amanda Jackson, and she is here to speak to you about her experience with domestic abuse."

Amanda Jackson faced us and smiled, revealing a mouth filled with huge gaps where teeth should have been. It was a shocking contrast to her elegance. Closing her mouth, she waited a beat before speaking.

"I'm going to need all new teeth," Amanda said. "That's what it took for me to finally leave a husband who had been beating me for years. This last time, he punched me at the top of the stairs. I fell all the way to the bottom."

"I spent three weeks in the hospital being treated for my injuries." She told us how she'd been married to an abusive man for ten years. Each time he hurt her, he would apologize. He always had some excuse: he'd just lost his job; he'd had too much to drink; or something she'd said reminded him of his unhappy childhood.

"Each time, his words tugged at my heartstrings and I took him back," she explained. "I always wanted to make things better for him, because that was what I was in the habit of doing."

CHAPTER 23

Her words made me think of Ty. I'd
empathized so much with the pain that had
caused him to explode with violence that I'd
paid no attention to my own hurt. I'd become
so used to caring for Ty that I'd forgotten how
to take care of myself.

"No matter how much you love a batterer,
someone who loses control and inflicts pain
on you, it's always better to leave," Amanda
Jackson concluded. "You don't deserve to be

hurt. Nothing you ever said or did warrants it, nothing, not ever. Love yourself enough to leave an abuser."

I sat there with my eyes shut, wanting to take her words into my mind, let them flow down into my heart.

So what if I had been too cheerful in the face of Ty's defeat? I had only been trying to help.

It didn't matter that I wouldn't get back into the car that night. I had a right to my anger and to do what I wanted.

But Ty had no right to hit me.

"A real man will never hit you," Amanda Jackson concluded. "And there's no reason to put up with a guy who does."

Tears brimmed in my eyes, but they were tears of relief and sprang from a new belief in myself. Nothing like this was ever going to happen to me again. I'd learned the hard way, but the important thing was that I *had* learned.

My next boyfriend would never, ever, lay a hand on me in anger.

About the Author

Suzanne Weyn has written many books for children and young adults. She holds a degree in teaching adolescents and has taught at New York University and City College of New York.